OLIVER
and the Noisy Baby

MARA BERGMAN ✳ NICK MALAND

Oliver Donnington Rimington-Sneep

was hoping and wishing the baby would sleep.

OLIVER

and the Noisy Baby

First published in 2011 by Hodder Children's Books
This paperback edition first published in 2012
Text copyright © Mara Bergman 2011 Illustration copyright © Nick Maland 2011
Hodder Children's Books, 338 Euston Road, London NW1 3BH
Hodder Children's Books Australia, Level 17/207 Kent Street, Sydney, NSW 2000

A catalogue record of this book is available from the British Library.

ISBN: 978 0 340 99746 8
10 9 8 7 6 5 4 3 2 1

Printed in China

Hodder Children's Books is a division of Hachette Children's Books, an Hachette UK Company
www.hachette.co.uk

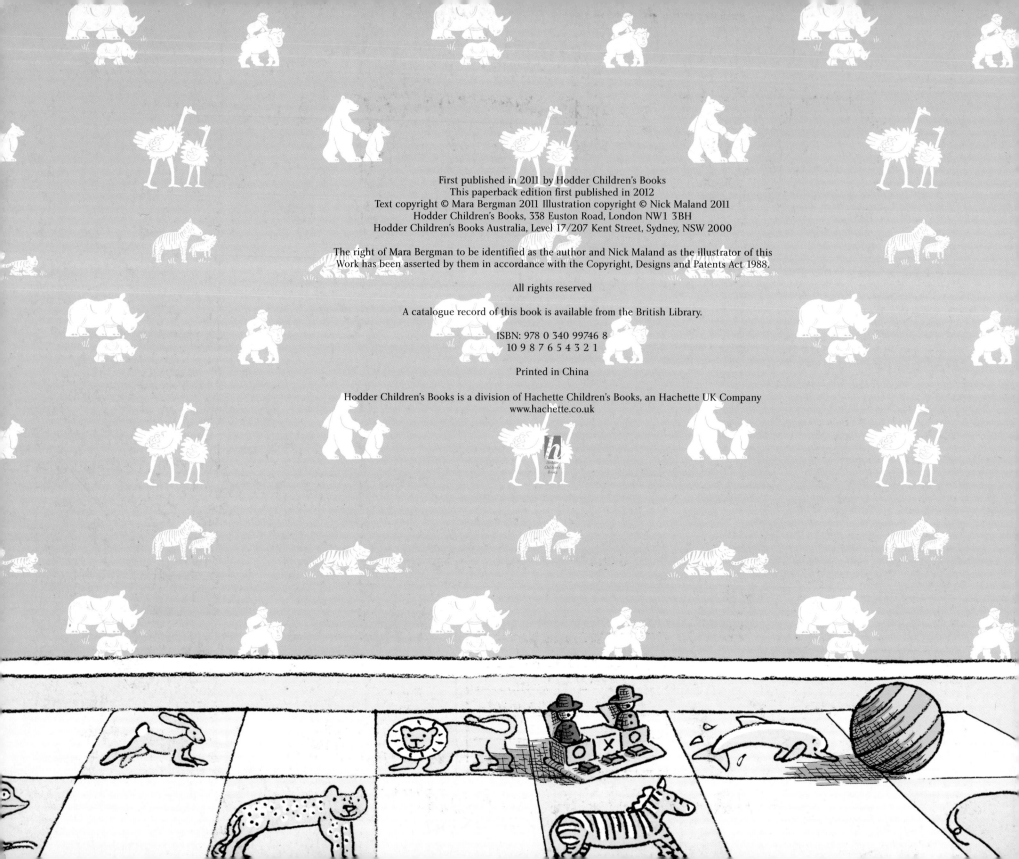

His parents were doing whatever they could
but **nothing** they tried seemed to do any good.

She cried all day long, she cried the night through.

Oliver thought he might start to cry too!

He reached for his plane
and he opened the door.

He sat down inside,
got the engines to roar…

and he flew!

Up, up, over lamp-posts and buildings and crowds,
way up in the air, in the sky, through the clouds...

to a freezing cold land,
full of ice, full of snow,
where polar bears lived
and trees couldn't grow.

Bears skated and swam, bears fished in the sea,

but Oliver started to shiver so he...

got back in his plane and he flew!

Oliver hadn't seen zebras before,
or ostriches, cheetahs, rhinos, and more.
Everywhere animals grazed in the sun –
when all of a sudden...

they started to run!
Oliver thought he had better leave too, so he...

got back in his plane and he flew!

Oliver hadn't seen leopards before,
and he longed to see monkeys

and hear tigers roar.

Then he yawned and he watched
while they settled at night,
mums, dads and young ones
as they cuddled tight.

But someone was crying –
who could it be?
Oliver wondered,
'Does the baby want me?'

Straight away Oliver knew what to do!
He hopped in his plane, he took off...

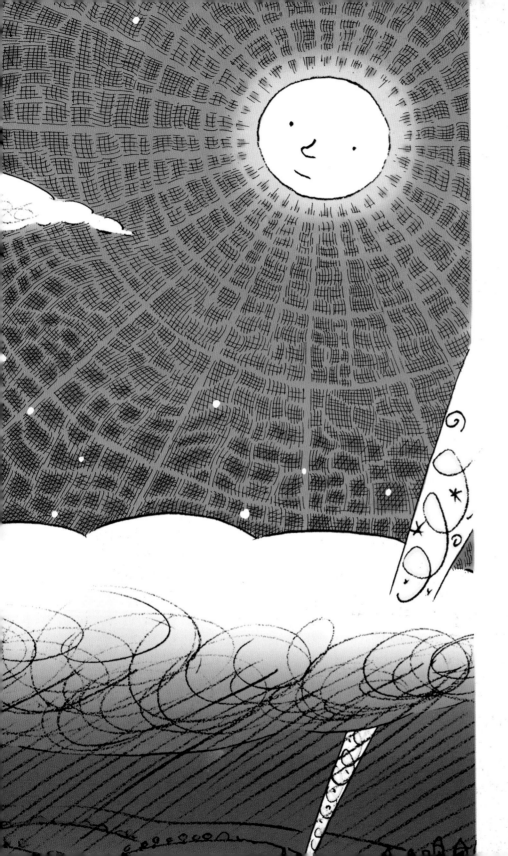

through the skies and the clouds
to his home far away
to the place he loved best
at the end of each day.

Waiting for him were
his mum, dad and sister.

He picked up the baby,
he hugged her and kissed her

and made her stop crying and told her he'd missed her...

and Oliver Donnington Rimington-Sneep
huddled and cuddled the baby to sleep.